# Dear Parent:

Congratulations! Your child is taking the first steps on an exciting journey. The destination? Independent reading!

**STEP INTO READING®** will help your child get there. The program offers books at five levels that accompany children from their first attempts at reading to reading success. Each step includes fun stories, fiction and nonfiction, and colorful art. There are also Step into Reading Sticker Books, Step into Reading Math Readers, and Step into Reading Phonics Readers— a complete literacy program with something to interest every child.

## Learning to Read, Step by Step!

**Ready to Read  Preschool–Kindergarten**
• big type and easy words • rhyme and rhythm • picture clues
For children who know the alphabet and are eager to begin reading.

**Reading with Help   Preschool–Grade 1**
• basic vocabulary • short sentences • simple stories
For children who recognize familiar words and sound out new words with help.

**Reading on Your Own  Grades 1–3**
• engaging characters • easy-to-follow plots • popular topics
For children who are ready to read on their own.

**Reading Paragraphs  Grades 2–3**
• challenging vocabulary • short paragraphs • exciting stories
For newly independent readers who read simple sentences with confidence.

**Ready for Chapters  Grades 2–4**
• chapters • longer paragraphs • full-color art
For children who want to take the plunge into chapter books but still like colorful pictures.

**STEP INTO READING®** is designed to give every child a successful reading experience. The grade levels are only guides. Children can progress through the steps at their own speed, developing confidence in their reading, no matter what their grade.

Remember, a lifetime love of reading starts with a single step!

*for Sophia Harvey*

*She may be small,*
*but she is strong.*
*Her hair is red.*
*Her cat is Long!*

Copyright © 1999 by Jon Buller and Susan Schade. All rights reserved under International and Pan-American Copyright Conventions. Published in the United States by Random House Children's Books, a division of Random House, Inc., New York, and simultaneously in Canada by Random House of Canada Limited, Toronto. Originally published by Golden Books, an imprint of Random House Children's Books, a division of Random House, Inc., New York, in 1999.

www.stepintoreading.com

Educators and librarians, for a variety of teaching tools, visit us at
www.randomhouse.com/teachers

*Library of Congress Cataloging-in-Publication Data*
Schade, Susan.
Cat on the mat / by Susan Schade and Jon Buller.
    p.   cm. — (Step into reading. A step 2 book)
SUMMARY: Cat dreams of being on the gymnastics team and spends all summer learning to tumble and flip.
ISBN 0-307-26207-3 (trade) — ISBN 0-375-99989-2 (lib. bdg.)
[1. Cats—Fiction.   2. Gymnastics—Fiction.   3. Stories in rhyme.]
I. Buller, Jon, 1943– .   II. Title.   III. Series: Step into reading. Step 2 book.
PZ8.3.S287   Cat   2004   [E]—dc21   2002015235

Printed in the United States of America   12  11  10  9  8  7  6  5  4
First Random House Edition

STEP INTO READING, RANDOM HOUSE, and the Random House colophon are registered trademarks of Random House, Inc.

STEP INTO READING®  STEP 2

# Cat on the Mat

by Susan Schade
and Jon Buller

Random House New York

Cat lives at home.

She has pink socks,
two posters, and
three lucky rocks.

Her father paints.

Her mom writes books.

Her sister sings.

Her brother cooks.

Cat hangs around.
She's in the way.

She wonders what
to do all day.

She visits Rat.

They sit and talk.

They watch TV.

They take a walk.

This looks like fun.

Rat wants to try.

Cat isn't sure.

She feels too shy.

The coach is nice
to Cat and Rat.

He lets them tumble
on the mat.

They join a class.

They learn to flip.

Sometimes they bump.

Sometimes they slip.

Cat sees a mat.
She has a dream.
She dreams of being
on the team.

Cat may be small,
but she is strong.

She works and works,
all summer long.

The big day comes.

Cat runs. She pounces.

She twists and lands.

Oops! Extra bounces.

It's Rabbit's turn.
She leaps! She soars!

She nails it, and
she gets good scores.

Chick mounts the bars.
She swoops. She swings.

She points her toes,
and spreads her wings.

Cat's swing is slow.

Her swoop is small.

She tries her best.

She does not fall.

Rat is so cool
on balance beam.

You know that she
will make the team.

But Cat is nervous,
and it shows.
She wobbles
on a simple pose.

The floor event
comes after beam.
It's Cat's last chance
to make the team.

The music makes her
tap her feet.

When Cat is good,
she's hard to beat.

Cat on the mat!
Watch her go!
Twenty-one handsprings
in a row!

Hooray for Rabbit,
Chick, and Rat!
They made the team—
And so did Cat!